Little Tree Found

Story by
Troy Schmidt

Illustrations by
Rob Corley and
Chuck Vollmer

KIDS

Nashville, Tennessee

Deep in the woods, where few people go,
Lived a young Little Tree that wanted to grow.
Little Tree looked to the heavens on high
And longed to be tall, to see the world from the sky.

He asked the tall trees, "Would you be my friend?
Let's hang out sometime. Just let me know when."
He greeted the animals that passed him by
And tried to make friends with a cheerful "hi."

But no one talked back or seemed to care.
Most just grunted like an angry ol' bear.
Little Tree wondered what he should do
To make a good friend or three or two.

Wrapped in his needles was a thin, sticky web,
The home of a cranky, old spider named Jeb.
Ol' Jeb had once lived way up high in the trees.
Little Tree begged him, "Be my friend,
    won't you please?"

"What's the use?" Jeb said,
Letting out a huge sigh.
"Trees come and go,
No matter how hard you try.
The little ones get lost
In this world so big.
You'll never be nothing
But a tiny ol' twig."

"There has to be someone in the world who cares;
There has to be someone who can hear my prayers."
He looked up to the sky and hoped for much more
And reached out his branches until they were sore.

Next day, Little Tree felt a tremble in the ground;
Way off in the distance he heard a strange sound.
"Maybe it's the friends that I prayed would soon come."
But what he saw then made him frightened and numb.

Men carried big tools and
chopped down big trees,
Then threw them in trucks
with the greatest of ease.
Jeb pounced from his web,
his eight legs in high gear.
"See you later, Little Tree!
I'm out of here!"

They cut down the trees
both large and small,
But yanked Little Tree
from the ground, roots and all.
They threw him in the back,
with trees in a stack.
Then his world went blurry
and slowly . . . pitch black.

His senses returned, and Little Tree could see
That this was a bad place, a bad place indeed.
The trees all around him shivered and shook.
Little Tree closed his eyes, not wanting to look.

Crackling and crashes and cries filled the air—
The sounds shook his roots, gave him quite a scare.
The smoke and the filth made him cough and wheeze;
He longed for a breath of a cool, forest breeze.

Where am I? he wondered, his insides quite dry.
When will I see home? How did I get here and why?
What is this awful place that fills me with fear?
Then down his branch rolled, not dew, but a tear.

Days went on, and Little Tree was alone,
As others departed to places unknown.
Lost and hurting, filled with worry and strife,
He soon needed water, the water of life.

As the night came and a snow began to fall,
Little Tree gave up hope he would leave these four walls.
His branches were sagging, and his trunk had frozen.
Time had run out as the doors began closing.

Then out of the darkness and into the light
Stepped two friendly creatures,
a most welcomed sight.
One was the father and the other, his son,
But they walked together as if they were one.

The owner said, "Sorry, not much left to buy,
Just this one tiny tree, about knee high.
He's small and dying, headed right for the trash,
Unless someone buys him. We take check or cash."

Little Tree cried, "Take me home with you now.
I give you my life, my branches I bow.
There's nothing I can do to save me from death.
I give you my all with my last dying breath."

The son paused a moment, then knew what to do.
"Let's take him home and make him shiny and new,
For this small Christmas tree feels quite sad and lost.
But I'll pay the price, no matter what the cost."

Christmas, the tree thought,
I've not heard of before,
But it will be a time that I love and adore,
For I have been rescued from dying and death
And given a new life, a new chance, new breath.

The sound of singing and the ringing of bells
Told the waking Little Tree that all was well.
His branches now sparkled with lights, white and bright,
While the living water helped him reach new heights.

Little Tree no longer wanted to cry.
He knew while he lived here, he never would die.
He now had a family of sisters and brothers
In a field of gold with room for many others.

The story does not end
for our Little Tree:
He grew in a place
where he always felt free,
For once he was lost,
and now he is found;
He made his home where
it's Christmas year 'round.

Adults, after you read the story, talk to your children about what the story means. Here are questions to prompt discussion and answers you want to listen for.

QUESTION: At the beginning of the story, what did the Little Tree want?
ANSWER: He wanted a friend. He wanted someone to care about him.

QUESTION: What happened to the Little Tree when the trucks arrived?
ANSWER: Little Tree was pulled out of the ground and taken to the tree lot. He began to die.

QUESTION: How did the Little Tree feel?
ANSWER: Lost. All alone. Afraid.

QUESTION: Why did the Little Tree begin to die?
ANSWER: It did not have healthy roots or water for life.

QUESTION: Who found him?
ANSWER: The Father and Son.

QUESTION: What did the Little Tree do when he saw the Father and Son?
ANSWER: He called out to them for help. He wanted to go with them.

QUESTION: How did the Father and Son get the tree?
ANSWER: They bought him. They paid a price.

QUESTION: What did they do to the Little Tree when they got it home?
ANSWER: They decorated him and gave him water. They promised to take care of him forever. They planted him in a field with other trees.

QUESTION: How did the Little Tree feel now?
ANSWER: Brand new. Loved. He had hope. He no longer wanted to cry.

QUESTION: Did the Little Tree want to go anywhere else after that?
ANSWER: No. He loved his new home with the Father and the Son.

The story of Little Tree tells the story of Christmas. We are alone and need help, so God sent his son to the earth at Christmas to be with us. We desire relationship and God wants us to have that relationship with him. He saves us if we just call out to him for help.

The book says: "For this Christmas tree feels quite sad and lost.
But I'll pay the price, no matter what the cost."

The Bible says: But God demonstrates His own love toward us,
in that while we were yet sinners, Christ died for us.—*Romans 5:8*

The book says: "He soon needed water, the water of life."